I0782221

FREE TO FASHION

A collection of stories about being Free to Fashion
from Birrong Girls High School and Bossley Park High School.

Story
FACTORY

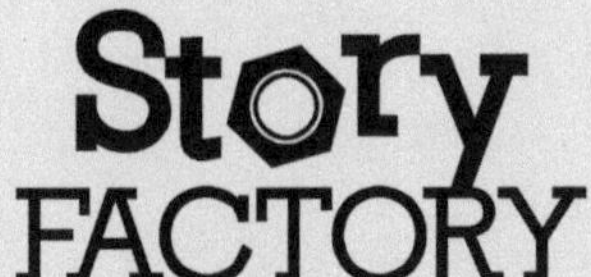

First published in 2024

Story Factory
www.storyfactory.org.au

ABN 71 645 321 582

176 Redfern Street, Redfern
Gadigal Land, NSW 2016 Australia

90 George Street, Parramatta
Burramattagal Land, NSW 2150 Australia

ISBN 978-1-922719-34-8

Cover illustration and design by Chatchakonrak Promchan
Edited by Purnima Mahesh and Elizabeth Arrigo
Typeset and interior design by Cassandre Collins
Photographs by Edwina Pickles, Thuy Giang, Sonya Price-Kelly and Natalie Goodes
Printed in Australia by IngramSpark

Story Factory acknowledges the Traditional Custodians of the Lands on which we work and live. We pay our respects to Elders past and present and extend that respect to all Aboriginal and Torres Strait Islander peoples.

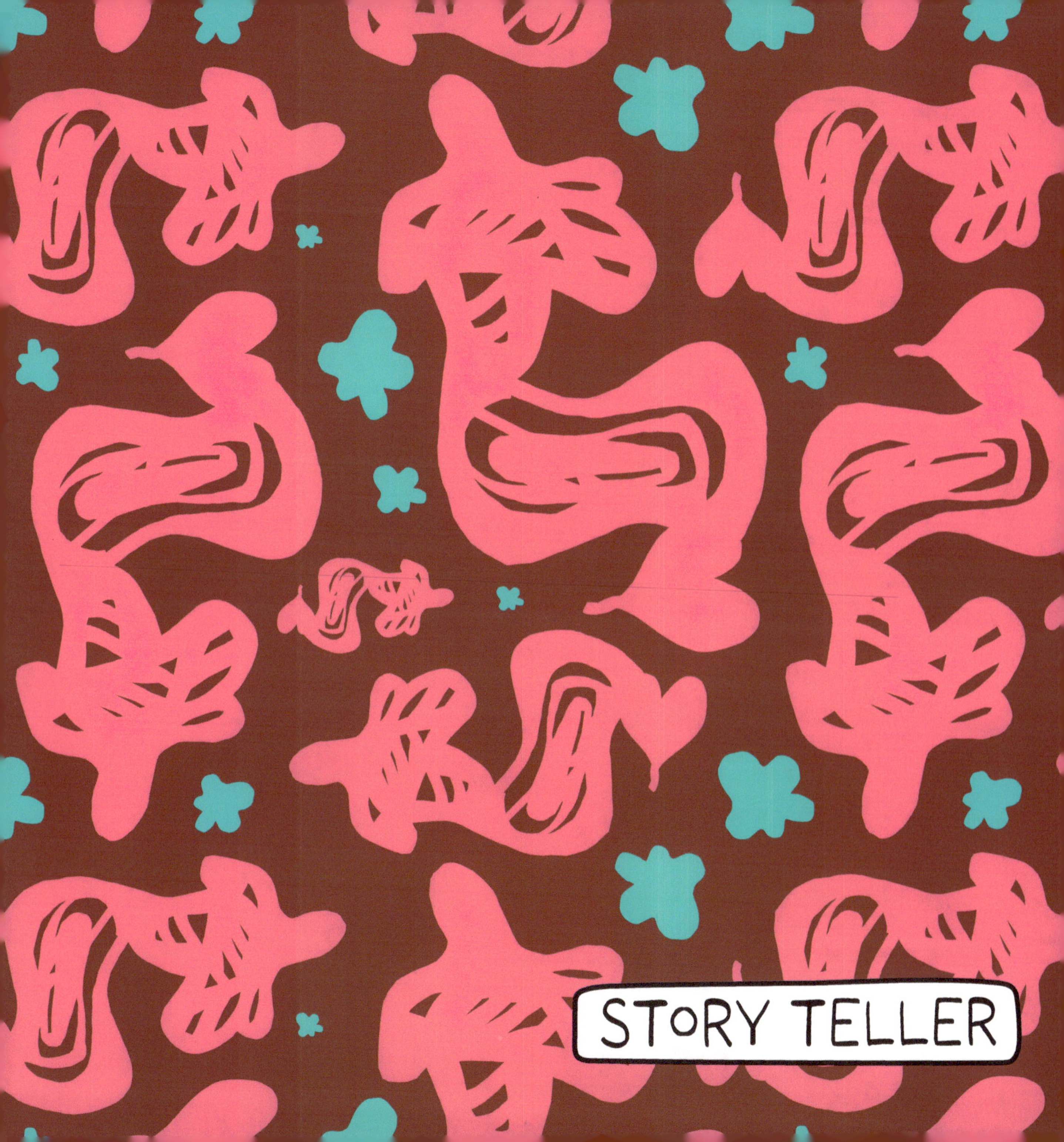
STORY TELLER

FREE TO FASHION

In 2024, Story Factory collaborated with The Social Outfit to deliver a unique project to amplify the voices of young women from Birrong Girls and Bossley Park high schools in Western Sydney.

Students met refugee and new migrant women who are trained by, and employed at, The Social Outfit, as well as the dedicated team operating the organisation. The students, sewing technicians, artists and storytellers explored fashioning as it relates to identity, culture and self-expression. The young women shared their ideas and wrote a range of stories.

The students explored these topics further with artistic facilitators Issy Parker, Chatchakonrak Promchan and Sonya Price-Kelly who supported them to create physical artforms: ceramic formations, pastel and marker drawings. The culmination of these diverse creations was the inspiration for internationally renowned textile artist, Clementine Barnes, to bring to life two unique fabric designs: "Amplify," printed on 100 per cent silk and a screen print, "Story Teller," printed on cotton sateen and linen. The skilled creatives and sewing technicians at The Social Outfit designed and manufactured a one-of-a-kind garment using these two prints. The garments, fabric prints, publication and artworks created during the project were displayed in a dedicated exhibition during The Social Outfit's 10th birthday celebration in September 2024 at Carriageworks in Eveleigh, Sydney.

The students' storytelling and musings demonstrate their strong connection to culture and identity. The young women celebrate their individuality and imagine their futures. Their written words sit alongside the rich imagery of the project in this publication, *Free to Fashion.*

Story FACTORY

Story Factory is a not-for-profit creative writing organisation, running programs for young people aged 7-17. We run programs in under-resourced communities in Sydney and digitally across Australia.

Supported by our community of expert educators and volunteer tutors, young people are empowered to create stories of all kinds, which we share and celebrate. At Story Factory we know that by building writing skills, we help young people develop creativity and the confidence to find their voices and shape their futures.

TONY BRITTEN

Tony Britten is a Sydney-based English teacher who has taught in secondary schools and arts organisations. He presents regularly at state and national education conferences. Tony has taught creative writing at Story Factory in a range of roles since 2016 and is currently a Storyteller Manager. He loves creating opportunities for students to explore the chemistry between writing and the visual arts.

NITA VAN DEN BOOGAARD

Nita is an English Teacher with over 20 years' experience teaching in South Western Sydney. She joined Story Factory as a Storyteller Manager in 2024. Nita has a passion for igniting creativity in young people and empowering them to understand the ways they learn best and their creative processes. She works to create an open, fun learning environment where the student voice is central and a range of creative approaches are valued.

THE SOCIAL OUTFIT

The Social Outfit is a fashion label with a difference. We support refugee and new migrant women to kick-start their Australian careers. We believe in an Australia where refugees and new migrants are warmly welcomed and settle well, celebrating our diversity, collective skills and strengths.

Founded in 2014, we are a registered charity operating a work integration social enterprise. We aim to support women in launching their Australian careers. We create ethical, sustainable fashion that is celebratory by design, showcasing the skills, creativity and strengths of refugee and migrant women. We do this through our retail clothing store and ethical manufacturing workroom in Sydney's Inner West. Eighty-five per cent of our garments are also made from fabric diverted from landfill, saving over 14 tonnes to date.

The Social Outit's sewing team creates beautiful pieces across apparel, homewares and accessories, producing items of the highest quality. The Social Outfit's sewing team and workroom were a source of inspiration to the students engaged in the Free to Fashion project.

CHATCHAKONRAK PROMCHAN

Chatchakonrak Promchan is a Sydney-based emerging artist who is also a talented sewing technician working for The Social Outfit. Her practice has developed from illustrations of herself and is inspired by her travels and daily life. Her style portrays fundamental artistic elements through dots, lines and other forms. By using monochrome colour schemes her pieces avoid expression through colour, instead drawing a focus to each illustration's composition and details.

ISSY PARKER

Issy Parker is a Sydney-based practising and exhibiting artist, and ceramic teacher to both adults and children. Her practice deliberately and carefully embodies the play between intent and surrender. Her works seek to celebrate individuality and diversity, and explore the balance between nature's process and the artist's hand to organically create lively and distinct vessels.

CLEMENTINE BARNES

Clementine is an Australian artist currently living and working in France. Her artistic practice explores the relationship between storytelling, craft and healing. Artist-in-residence at the Cité internationale des arts in Paris since June 2024, she is busy experimenting in the ceramics studio; making objects for a future project she hopes won't break in the kiln!

Clementine first collaborated with The Social Outfit in 2020 on the Heirloom Community print. She is absolutely delighted to have the opportunity to team up with The Social Outfit again in 2024 to create the Free to Fashion community prints, alongside artist Issy Parker and Story Factory for The Social Outfit's 10th anniversary.

Learn more about Clementine and her practice at www.clementinebarnes.com

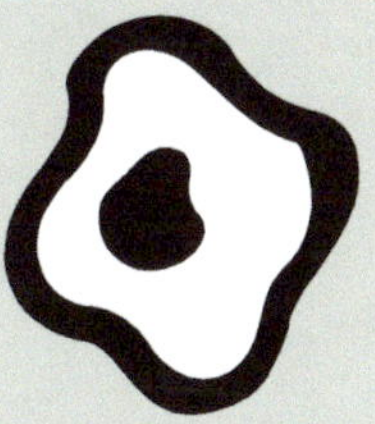

mountains are cal
e the best dreams
ories life is shor
list and so the a
n, and time is ne
the last time you
roam i want a li

An aspect of Free to Fashion that I enjoyed was the numerous creative activities, specifically working with clay, because that was so hands-on and stimulating.

Through Free to Fashion, I was able to see the inside of a fashion warehouse and manufacturing space, and see how slow fashion is created.

To me, being free to fashion means being able to express myself and my Islamic beliefs through what I wear. Being free to fashion means I am able to be modest yet fashionable.

STRANGER

During an icebreaker, I had asked a stranger what her favourite colour was. She replied with 'black', and I responded with 'why?' What could be so appealing about that colour that you would prefer it over all the others? What my nine-year-old brain had failed to comprehend is that although black is well . . . bleak, it has the unique ability to embody elegance and complement every other colour. Looking back at it now, that stranger with the wide hazel eyes and toothy grin became one of my very best friends for the very reason that she was the essence of what it means to be the colour black; to be a blend of the brightest colours yet the darkest shade.

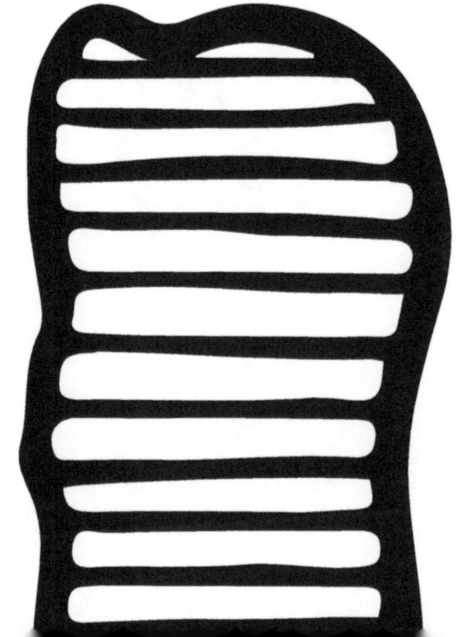

SPECTRUM

What colour represents me? Am I an ocean blue or a princess pink? Does the colour green make my chocolate-coloured eyes pop or should I play it safe and wear all black? My mother says the colour purple suits me, my sister thinks gold velvety fabric makes my skin tone shine. My cousin says sage-green dresses make me look older, and my brother says red silk makes me look like royalty. My father sees me as a little girl when I wear baby pink, and my friends say light blue complements the rosy pink of my cheeks. I cannot picture a single colour that captures my chaotic personality, beauty, and character. What other people see when they look at me and how I see myself change as I grow, and my colours change with me.

I am not one colour.

Whether I am wearing red, green, pink or blue, or I am seven, ten or 15 years old, I will always be a mixture of bright colours and vibrant pigments.

I am a spectrum.

THOBES

Black embroidered fabric. Red jewels hand-sewn. Chiffon sleeves. Olive green trim and orange embroidered flowers. My aunties sit on floor cushions, surrounded by Turkish tea cups and ka'ak. Their hands buoyed up, their mouths full. Gossip and chatter, chai and biscuits. Needles and satin fabrics flood the living room as they sit and cross-stitch their hearts into the black sleeves. Each Palestinian thobe conveys where we come from, our favourite fruits, and how old we are. Maifa, Raha, Gaza. Juicy olives and citrusy oranges. Five, 17, 25, 60. I stand proud, wearing my heart on my sleeve and my land on my back. Each thread on this dress weaves the web of my confidence. You cannot undermine my thobe. You cannot undermine this power.

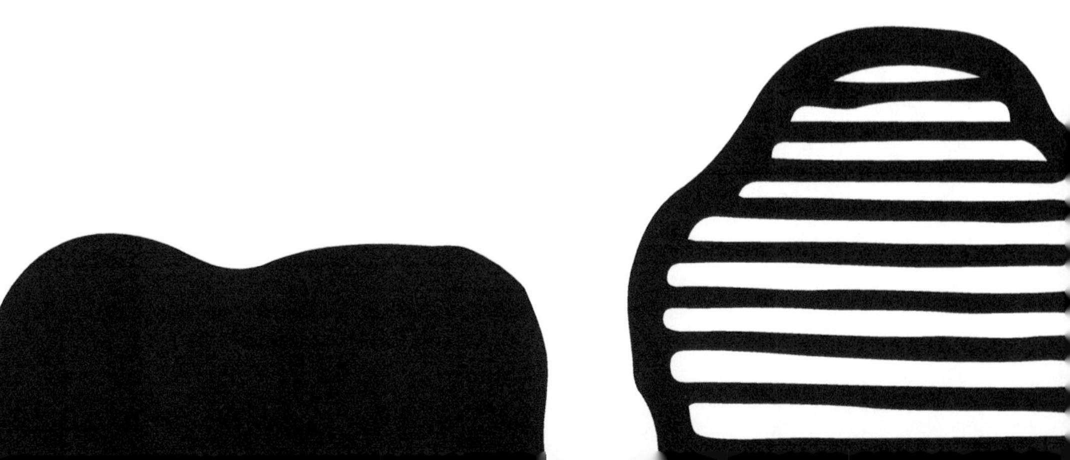

An aspect of Free to Fashion that I enjoyed was travelling to The Social Outfit and watching the behind-the-scenes of textile production. I saw all different types of sewing machines and workstations. It was an inspiring experience. I also learned how textile workstations are organised for efficiency. It was a system of workers in a production line.

To me, being free to fashion means that working with textiles is an art form that can take any shape or form. Free to fashion means that fashion has no limits and can be anything we want it to be.

My signature colour is light blue. Most things that I own, like jeans, jumpers and scarves, are blue.

GRANDMA'S TREASURE

My grandma loved jewels. Not the small dainty kind. No. My grandma lived by the phrase 'Go big or go home.' Emeralds, diamonds, her eyes would glitter like a magpie in the wind when they'd sparkle in the market windows. Exquisite, elaborate, opulent. That's how she'd describe them. Like they were the most elegant, refined pieces of art she owned. She'd wear them everywhere, and anywhere they could be seen— piercings, bracelets, rings, necklaces. Their brilliant shimmer would always catch the light. We'd always know when she entered a room; she glowed like a goddess. Soon enough, jewellery wasn't enough to satisfy her. It fed into a new hobby. My grandma would sit by the window as she sewed her most prized possessions into her clothes. Every garment she could get her hungry hands on was embellished with treasure. When she passed, I inherited her robe. 'Majestic' couldn't graze the surface of how precious it was. Smooth, rich, velvety fabric splattered with a cascade of glimmering jewels. It was beautiful. It was her. Bright, warm, comforting. My grandma sewed a piece of herself into her robe. My robe.

BEACH DAY

My heart thumps as I skip along the dusted horizon, wind weaving through my flowy scarves. Sand sifts through my toes, the air is salty and crisp. Another family beach day. I'm excited. Whenever we host a beachy get-together, my uncle never fails to send shockwaves through the family. You see, he loves his hats. Big hats, small hats, wide hats, narrow hats, PATTERNED hats, he doesn't discriminate. On our last trip at Windang Beach, he arrived in a vibrant cerulean contraption. It had a wide circular base, a slim middle, and an even wider top. It was outrageously disproportionate and flashy with its cobalt-coloured add-ons, but he didn't seem to mind. A wide, sheepish grin was imprinted on his face, making him look about ten years younger. His hats made him happy, which made my family happy, so we played along. The younger kids made it a sort of competition, a guessing game if you will. Whoever could predict the type of hat he would show up in got bragging rights for the rest of the week. I've finally arrived at where my family's unpacked. The anticipation is basically tangible. Children cross their fingers and parents suck in their breaths. I clutch my phone. His hat's worth the wait.

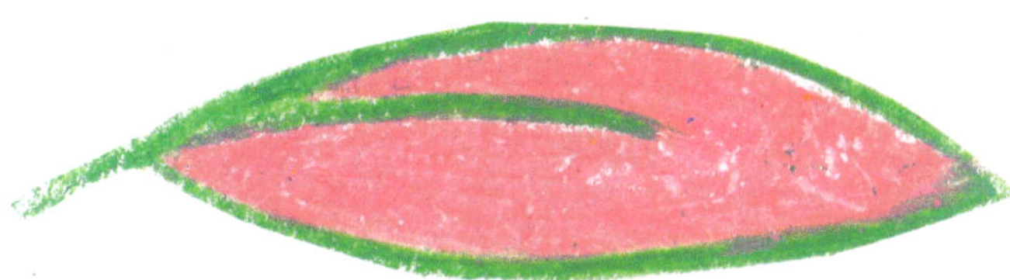

SUMMER SALES

Spices permeate the air as locals flock to surround the auctions at the Tripoli markets. I'm squeezed between multiple bodies, struggling to inhale the humid summer breeze. A warm hand envelops mine. It feels like comfort. It feels like safety. Jewels of every colour, shape and length hang from a stand. They sparkle, and the crowd sighs in awe as the shopkeeper spins them round and round like a carousel. I'm not looking at them. Her eyes, my grandma's eyes, sparkle. They shimmer as she looks down at me, as she smiles at me. 'Hundred,' she screams. 'We'll take it for a hundred.'

Surprised, the shopkeeper yelps with glee, slamming his hammer and sealing the deal.

On the way back to her apartment, my grandma stops to adorn me with her new purchase. A string of pearls that dangle like the branches of an olive tree. My grandfather's olive tree.

My heart splinters with joy, tears running down my face.

Now, in Australia, where we grow eucalyptus trees, not olives, I remember her. I remember her spark, her smile, her laugh. I remember home.

Her signature colours are black and white as they are easily pairable with outfits and go better with everything. She always wears comfortable clothing. The fashion item that best defines her is jewellery. You would never catch her wearing leather pants. Fashion enables her to express the way she wants to look, the things she enjoys and finds beautiful.

The fashion items she remembers from her childhood are bright and colourful, full of beautiful florals.

If she could change the world of fashion, she would contribute to the people who make our fashion wearable today, help enhance the fashion world, and make it enjoyable for the workers and customers.

Sally is a Year 10 student at Bossley Park High School. The aspect of Free to Fashion that she enjoyed was working together with the women from The Social Outfit—learning about their background and the work they do.

Something new she tried was working with ceramics for fashion. She enjoyed learning new concepts of fashion, colours, and fabrics.

To her, being free to fashion means expressing yourself through fashion. Your ideas and concepts. What you want to show off to the world. To her, being free to fashion means being proud and joyful about ways you express yourself through fashion.

She admires changing outfits—adding, taking away, editing. Her future self will be more colourful, with different accessories, more complex designs and materials together.

She would never wear overly sweet perfume.

WONDER

I walked into my parents' room and saw my mother going through the closet, putting clothes away, taking clothes out, organising the pants, dresses, suits, shirts and more into their own places. All the fabrics, colours, patterns flowing, radiating, and my mind started to wonder if I had any old clothes. So I asked her: 'Do I have any clothes from when I was little?'

'Well, not many, I guess,' she replied.

'Why didn't you keep them?" I asked.

She went silent for a moment.
'I couldn't. We had to leave.'

RELIEF

My place of freedom is a wonderful place, full of space for me to explore. It is a place where only I am allowed. When I'm in that space, everything is okay, there are no problems, nothing I don't enjoy. A place of no consequences, just exploration. It is all open, outdoors, with only nature and beautiful sculptures of expression. It's like looking at art. Something so calming it puts you at peace. Something so wonderful you could shed tears of joy and relief. My place is a dream. You can hear water trickling, and sun glistening. The wind slowly wraps around you, holding you, so you can appreciate the beautiful, extraordinary surroundings and openness.

SHAMES

An aspect of Free to Fashion that I enjoyed was writing and expressing my thoughts.

Something I learned from Free to Fashion was to look at things from a different perspective.

To me, being free to fashion means being able to express yourself.

You would never catch me wearing bright, tight clothing.

You will always find me wearing very wide black clothing, a face veil and a floor-length abaya that covers my head.

The fashion item I remember from my childhood is a headband that said 'Ya Hussain'!

If I could change the world of fashion, I would create a large variety of long and modest clothing.

MY ABAYA MY IDENTITY

When she enters with her black clothing, it gives her power. The black reflects her seriousness, reflects her modesty, reflects her, and reflects her choices.

Like a shadow not wanting to be seen, hiding and watching your every move, she wears it like our ancestors, who stood in the face of oppression, when truth was alone, alone and sad.

The bottom of her abaya brushing against the grass, her shoulders up. She walks like a man not wanting the evil eyes to turn to look at her. Her black veil covers the light that glows from her face, her scarf pulled down to cover her eyebrows, showing only her eyes, allowing her to only look one way and find nothing more beautiful than the prayer mat laid out and waiting to reconnect her with her creator.

THE SECRET OF THE MARBLE

Cold between my warm hands is a block of marble broken off from the walls of the shrine in Karbala, Iraq.

Its pale colour, matching my skin. The streaks of red gliding through it, looking as if a vein burst. The green streak that dances beside the red symbolises life and freedom. But altogether, it reminds of the death of the great armless soldier who was buried beneath, the marble a symbol of a story that still awaits its revenge. Black, the abaya that was used to cover his body on the burning sands of Karbala. His sister, who stood in the face of oppression, who held on to her modesty even though the tents were burning all around her. She held on to her modesty and so will I, I will continue to carry the message of the slaughtered family of the prophet through my abaya.

Clothes aren't just materials: they're memories too, especially for Catalina, a Year 10 student at Bossley Park High School, who believes in the freedom of creativity and ideas, and expresses her confidence through creative art and writing.

You would never catch Catalina wearing double patterns, and always find her wearing jewellery and her signature colour: green. Green brings her joy and warmth, and makes her hazel eyes pop!

The fashion item that best describes Catalina is her hippie pants. The flow and colours express her personality whilst also being comfortable.

SHOPPING

Shopping. We either love it or dread it. I step
in and out of hundreds, thousands of shops.
My anxiety peaks: the tight dressing rooms,
constant staff checking on you and, most of all,
the feeling of disappointment when the zipper
doesn't reach . . .

Shopping is like rolling the dice. How many
chances do you get to roll and try again? I have
my mum by my side, encouraging me to keep
trying on piles and piles of dresses, just so I can
find comfort and confidence in one of them.

On to the next store, again and again and again.
The feeling of giving up hits me, until I look up
and see my prize piece right in front of me. A
beautiful dress that I can breathe in, fit in, and
love myself in.

A PIECE OF LOVE

A piece of clothing that represents
freedom to me is my flowy sage
green skirt. It has lots of colourful
flowers embroidered at the bottom.

This skirt means a lot to me as it
was handmade and because my
mum bought it for me. When I tried
it on, I fell in love with it. I felt the
wind rushing through it, which put
the biggest smile on my face.

My mum didn't have much money.
But when she saw me in it, and she
saw how in love I was with it, she
bought it with what little she had.
Knowing this makes me appreciate
this piece of clothing even more.

This isn't just a skirt. This is a piece
of love. The love that it was made
with, the love I felt in it, the love my
mum bought it with.

Amarnie, a Year 10 student at Bossley Park High School, liked being able to let her creativity run wild during the Free to Fashion workshops. She learnt to express herself through art. She is a passionate person and loves being able to express her personality through the clothes and jewellery she wears. Amarnie's signature colour is pink because it's pretty and suits her complexion. You would never catch Amarnie wearing her school jacket outside the school gates, YUCK! You will always find her wearing her gold-plated blue-crystal cross necklace, and she likes to complement her outfits with a scarf.

Her favourite fashion memories are of the blue Elsa dress from her childhood with the sparkly train and her Dora the Explorer shirt, which she still treasures.

If Amarnie could change one thing about the fashion world, she would make it so that fashion trends live forever.

HAPPY MEMORIES

The sound of laughing and playing with Dora the Explorer blasting in the background. Playing. Laughing. Dora on repeat. My whole childhood. Every time I pick up that little pink shirt, the memories come flooding back like a rush of adrenaline. Clothes aren't just pieces of material. They hold happy memories waiting to be freed.

WHAT TO WEAR?

As a woman in today's society, having to pick something to wear that everyone approves of is truly draining! Having to worry about others' judgements, about how they will view me instead of how I want to feel, dismisses my own comfort and confidence.

Sometimes I wish I could wear what I want without others telling me how I should or shouldn't dress. Fashion should be a way to express myself.

An aspect of Free to Fashion that I enjoyed was being creative with my designs.

Through Free to Fashion, I learned how fabrics and prints are made.

To me, being free to fashion means being free to make or wear what you want.

My signature colours are black or white, because I like basic neutral colours and they look better on me.

You would never catch me wearing cow print.

HIJAB

When I think about what it means to be free to fashion, I always think about the hijab. The style and culture behind the hijab is beautiful. Nearly every part of the body is covered. From her arms to her ankles, she is all covered. It all represents modesty. It is supposed to cover her beauty. No man should know what lies beneath it, except for her husband.

When I put it on, it made me feel special and closer to my religion and who I am. At first, it was hard to get used to it. I had to buy the right clothes (baggy, long sleeves and long pants) and the right hijab and find my right hijab style. Once I figured out all the tips and tricks, I felt true to myself. I felt free to fashion.

SHINY WHITE PEARLS

While looking through my mum's jewellery, I see all the different jewellery she has—silver, gold, diamond, bulky necklaces, shiny earrings . . . everything anyone would dream of. But then I see this beautiful white string of shiny pearls on a necklace that I have never seen her wear before. Each pearl is about the size of a pea, and it has an easy but unique clasp to open and close it.

'What's this?' I ask my mum. 'Can I have it?'

'No,' she says, while laughing like I said something impossible.

Eventually I forget about it.

A few months later, my mum walks up to me, holding something in her hand.
'Here you go, you can have it,' she says.

I thank her and kiss her.

'Did you know this necklace was the first anniversary gift your dad got for me?' she tells me.

After that moment, I wear this necklace every day and feel so happy and pretty in it, knowing it's a symbol of love between my mum and dad.

BLENDING IN

I go out to the shops to pick something up. I don't want to catch anyone's attention, so I dress plain. I get to the shops in my black track-pants and white shirt, just like everyone else around. I see someone wearing an all-black suit and another girl wearing a beige coat. As I continue walking, I suddenly stop as I look at this girl walking so confidently. She really stands out, and she's not afraid. I wonder what about her is making her pop, and then I realise it's the bright blue baggy jeans and oversized jacket that even has a hoodie! Just when I think it can't get any better, I notice the matching leather bag and gloves. It's interesting because over her gloves she also added rings. After all that, the oval black glasses just pull the look together.

That was my fashion moment. The colours, the tones, the shades, and the way she strutted across the road made that moment amazing.

An aspect of Free to Fashion that I enjoyed was creating a variety of shapes with pastel crayons and learning about all different types of fabrics and textiles.

Something I learned from Free to Fashion was how to create a colourful and bold pattern.

To me, being free to fashion means to be creative and to know you will always be accepted.

The fashion item that best defines me is my hijab. It defines me, my culture, my religion and my personality. I'm from Iraq and Algeria, and I'm a Muslim. I'm a fun person and very social.

You would never catch me wearing triangle pointy shoes. I despise them.

You will always find me wearing flowery or plain dresses, or fancy dresses. I love long dresses and wear them anywhere.

Something I would never wear again is a chiffon scarf. It's just not right for me.

The fashion item that represents my culture is a kaftan from Algeria. It means a lot to my culture and is beautiful.

THE RAINBOW

When I think about what it means to be free to fashion
our identity, I always think about my teacher Ms V.
She teaches technology and loves it. I love when she
is enthusiastic about posting photos on Instagram,
especially when she takes them. Whenever I think
about free to fashion, she comes to my mind because
she changes her hairdo every month. Pink, orange, red,
green, blue, purple. All the colours, she wears them
like a uniform. She is very confident. She never feels
ashamed. I am always surprised and wait eagerly for the
next colour. Me and my best friend have started betting
what colour she'll have next. Even when her hair colour
changes, her wolf cut stays the same. The wolf cut is
chunky and flowy. It represents her. Every colour is a
different mood, and her mood changes every month.
She feels free to fashion, which makes me happy.

THE ELEGANT DRESS

One day I was scrolling through Insta and found an amazing dress with my mum.
I asked her to check the shop, and WOW, it was so beautiful—the colour, the
patterns and even the design of the dress, everything.

Knock. Knock. Knock. Something came in the mail. My mum had bought it for me.

My heart was full of joy. I was so grateful. As I took it out, I squealed. The floral
pattern on the cream colour and the way it was made with such precision.

I have always loved this dress and always will.

BETHANY

Angel (Bethany) is a Year 10 student at Bossley Park High School. The aspect of Free to Fashion that she enjoyed most was seeing everyone's different cultures through their fashion. She learned more about abstract artworks and how they can be turned into patterns as part of this program. To her, being free to fashion means the ability to express herself freely, without fear.

Angel's signature colour would be a sorta pale forest green—her favourite pants are that colour and she won't go out without them! She has a lot of rings that she wears out to places, and she especially loves her silver ones. She just really likes silver jewellery in general. You will never catch her wearing a dress, at least not for casual events . . . well, not even for formal ones actually. And she always wears a jacket, no matter the season. Fashion enables her to express how she feels and, at the same time, how she *wants* to feel. If she wants to feel happy, she'll wear something she feels comfortable in.

If Angel could change the world of fashion she'd change the way people view beauty. Humans are very social creatures, so having a preference isn't a bad thing, but fashion as an industry depicts for people what is normal and what isn't.

MEMORIES

I was younger than young—maybe five years old at the time—and I remember seeing a photo of my aunties, by blood and otherwise, with my mum at her wedding. They were all wearing Laos clothing. My mum was wearing dark maroon with gold accents and a matching sash, while my grandparents and aunties wore a darker green with silver embroidery, making my mum stand out.

FINDING FREEDOM

I remember this one time when I was really angry and very young so when they left the door open, I walked to my local shops, a 10-15 minute walk from my house, to buy food with my Christmas money . . . I'm pretty sure it was spring rolls. And then I walked to a park that was hidden by a bunch of trees. It wasn't the act of running away from home as much as the fact of just eating alone in a peaceful environment that has stayed with me. Now whenever I feel angry, I walk to the park and eat. It is my way of feeling free.

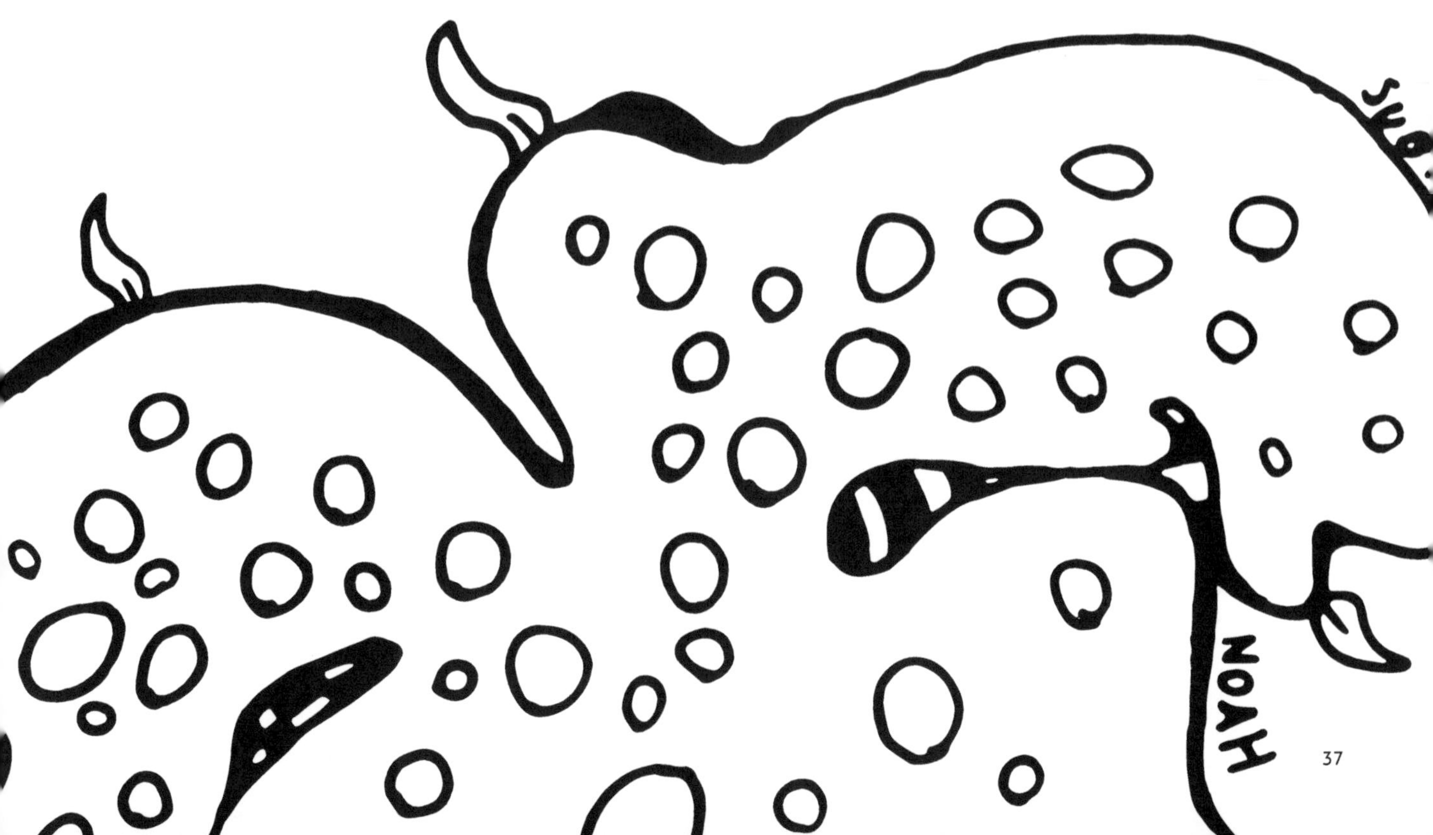

Manabba is a Year 10 student at Bossley Park High School. The aspect of Free to Fashion that she enjoyed was the writing, along with learning ceramic arts as part of this program. To her, being free to fashion means having the freedom to express yourself.

Her favourite colours are soft ones. And black. The fashion item that best defines her is boots and black leggings—she would even wear them at weddings if she were allowed! You would never catch her wearing skinny jeans. She always wears earrings and makeup, especially lip products. Fashion enables her to express her feminism.

An outfit she remembers from her childhood is a pink-and-white dress she wore with black shoes. The fashion item that represents her culture is the oversized clothes women wear—it allows them to be free and comfortable when cooking traditional food.

If she could change the world of fashion she would create more chances for her people to wear what they feel comfortable in. 'You are not supposed to fit clothes, clothes are supposed to fit you!' This is her philosophy of fashion.

FREEDOM

I felt free when I was watching the view of the sunset at the beach. It made me feel like I had escaped from the world and had my own world in which I could be alone. The smell of the beach, the sound of the waves, made me feel free. Being alone at the beach made me feel small, like there's this big space where you can be by yourself.

MY STYLE

The outfit that represents who I really am is baggy clothes with high boots. These clothes make me feel comfortable and confident, and represent my personality. Whenever I want to feel free, I love putting on lip liner with lip gloss—it makes me feel confident and feminine.

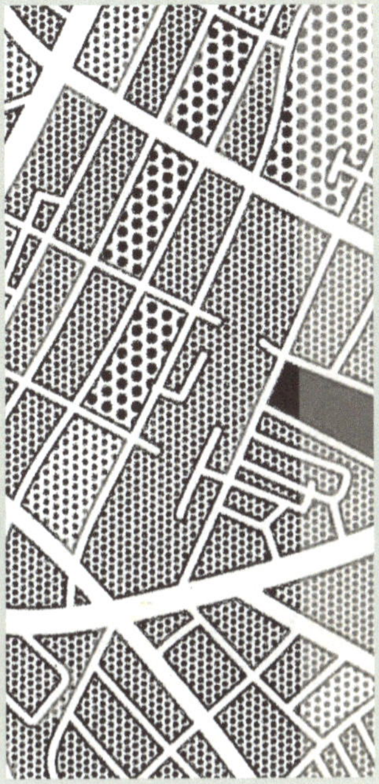

Nadeen is in Year 9 at Bossley Park High School. During the Free to Fashion project, she enjoyed finding out how the fashion industry works, and she loved working with clay. To Nadeen, being free to fashion means being free to express your personal style. Her signature colour is black, or darker colours. She chooses to dress modestly in dark shades, and you will always find her wearing mascara and her special cross necklace. Never neon colours! Nadeen is Chaldean, and she would love to wear the traditional blue and black dress called the khomala, with ornate silver belts and lots of sparkles. It is often worn for special celebrations.

KIDS' NIGHT

The time I feel freedom is when I am
home alone with my cousins.
It is a Saturday night and our parents
have all left to go out.
We can do anything we want: we
make food, watch movies, laugh and
share TikTok clips.
Freedom smells like popcorn and
tastes like KFC and pizza.
Freedom is a bowl full of warm
ramen and the giggles of my cousins.

THE CROSS

I love my cross necklace because
I got it from my aunty. It's a silver
necklace with diamonds forming the
cross. I got it when I was nine, and it's
a special memory of my aunty, who
doesn't live in Australia. It represents
my faith because Jesus died on the
cross for us. I never take it off.

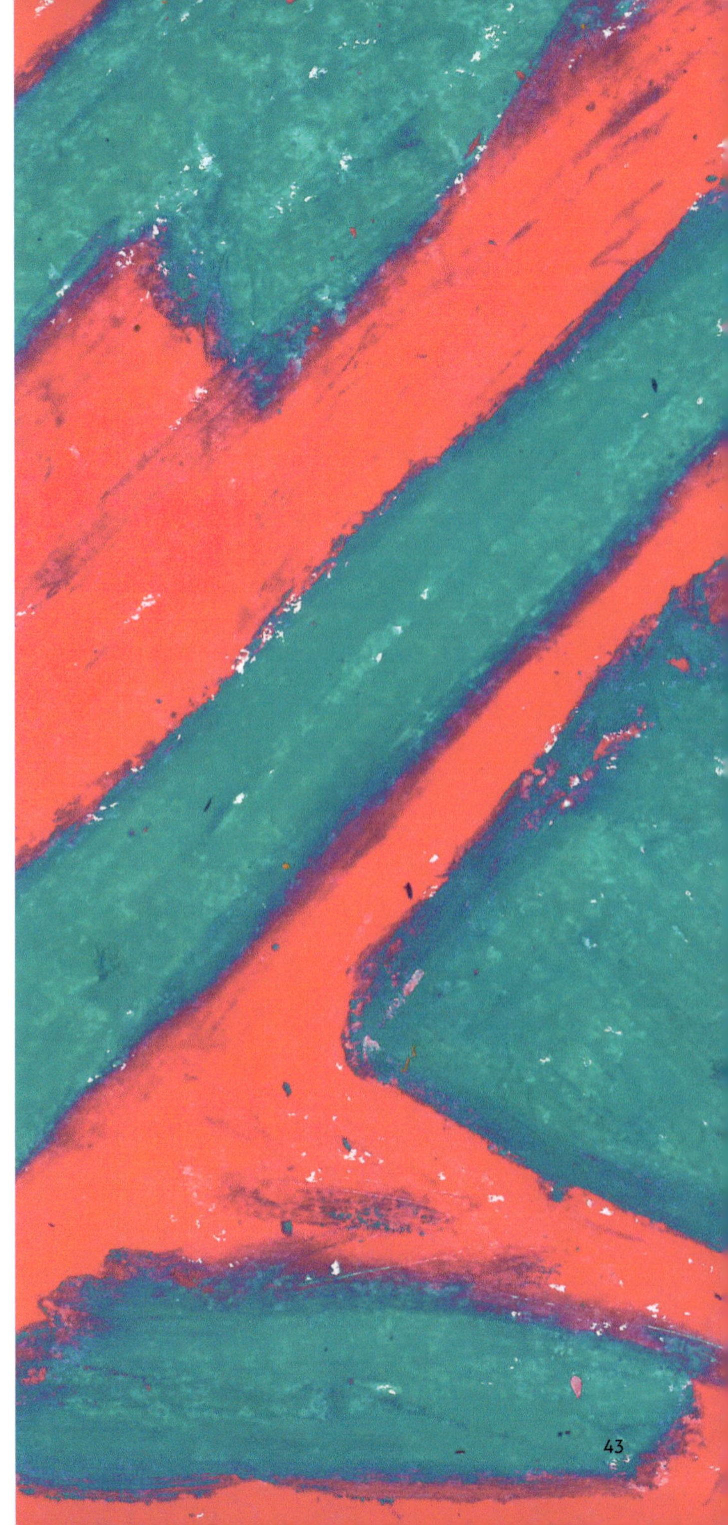

HAYLEY

Hey, hey! Hayley is a young girl with some magnificent dreams. She's all about expressing herself and knowing who she is, which is (when you say it out loud) a hard task to do. She doesn't even KNOW who she is yet, but she doesn't let that stop her trying. She's young and has her whole life to figure it out. For now, though, she's just happy being Hayley: a teenage girl who enjoys art and music.

BOW ON SHOW

When I was young, I would beg my mother to buy me JoJo bows. She was always confused by my obsession—all she saw were normal bows. But I saw more. The way the bows sparkled in the sun and popped with colour always made my mind explode with excitement. The silky bows made by a girl my age, and loved by so many. I would collect them and wear a different one every day. I'd smile so wide because the bows reminded me of a rainbow in a clear, crystal-blue sky. The smile of my childhood idol, JoJo Siwa, still sticks in my memory.

DISTANT DOVES

My cousin Chelsea and I were always close, so when her mother was soon to marry, we knew we had to work together to make everything perfect. That's probably why it was such a shock when we were asked to be flower girls and, more importantly, asked by the beautiful bride to wear white at her wedding. We all knew it was a weird request, but who were we to say no?

So on that day of bliss, we both wore these beautiful layered pearly white dresses. It's a fond memory, one I've always treasured. Recently, though, it became not much more than a memory as I lost that dress while moving houses. I was upset, angry at myself, for being so careless. And then, going through the stuff in our garage one day I found, hidden deep in a bag of my old clothes—the small white velvet dress! Just as beautiful after all those years. My eyes teared as my smile softened. I had finally found my fond memory.

SIENNA

Who is that student? It's Sienna! A Year 9 student proudly from Bossley Park. She loved the creative art component of Free to Fashion: drawing and working with clay.

To Sienna, being free to fashion means being able to wear anything she wants. That would ideally be motorcycle gear or suits.

Her favourite colours to wear include black, and earthy shades of brown and green. You will generally find her in a black turtleneck, light brown pants, a dark green coat and black combat boots, or in her rep team volleyball uniform.

Sienna believes that you aren't supposed to fit clothes, clothes are supposed to fit YOU.

NIGHTMARE

I strolled into the store, clothes everywhere, my mum by
my side. Everyone acting like seagulls scavenging among
the clothes racks. The workers wishing and begging to
go home. I was bored, I didn't want to be there. I dreaded
this, but mum insisted. I hate being outside: I'd rather be
at home eating or sleeping. Anything but this place.

'Come on, Sienna, just for a bit,' pleaded my mother.
'A bit? It's going to take hours . . .' I said with a huff.
(My mum takes so long looking for clothes and by the
time she finishes, I'm going to be an 89-year-old grandma
with three grandchildren and major back problems).

'Don't worry, we are looking for clothes for you,'
my mother said happily.

I stared at her. Even worse! Nothing fits my style, and
my mother's taste in clothes is terrible! I wanted to
skedaddle away in a hurry.

DANIEL DIAMOND

A costume that represents freedom
to me is a top hat with a red diamond
pattern because it belongs to the
character from my comic. He is a
detective, and I would love to be a
detective too! I created him: his name
is Daniel Diamond, he is 23 and loves
his friends, family, and solving crimes.

Reem is a Year 10 student at Bossley Park High School. The aspect of Free to Fashion that she enjoyed was being part of the process of creating artworks and designs that inspired the fabrics. She learned that fabrics can be creative and bright, expressive, quirky and cute. They don't have to be basic. To her, being free to fashion means opening up your mind and being free to think and do whatever you like, creating your own path and recognising your personality.

Her signature colour is a light blue mixed with white, and the fashion item that best defines her style is a modest but classy, long and flowy dress. As she is Muslim, you would never find her wearing a bikini! A hijab defines her and her religion.

As a child, she remembers wearing white dresses and nice little heels to family weddings.

Pieces of clothing that represent her culture are the hijab and the modest abaya, which are extremely significant as they represents her culture and faith.

PENCIL

I love shopping, especially when I'm with
my mum. We go everywhere together. We're
usually shopping for dresses, but only for Mum.

We step into a store, and suddenly I'm
shopping for myself!
'Basé in hame lebas dari,' Mum laughs.
'I don't have anything like this, though,'
I say in a sarcastic voice.

Mum tries on this dress in Modelle, and Dad's
with us. Dad is in love like the day they first
met. I feel jealous and decide 'I want some
dresses!' I try on this beautiful black dress,
and what does my dad say? 'Aynou khotar
daroomadi.' ('You look like a pencil.')
Mum laughs and I feel upset.

It's fine, I have many clothes at home and I
trust my parents' words. At least my mum
bought a dress she looked stunning in.

FASHION MY LIFE

My whole life, I've desperately wanted to be
a model or make my own clothes. I would see
people on the runway online and imagine that
one day that would be me walking the runway,
or that those would be MY designs the models
were wearing! I was inspired by my mum to
make my own clothes.

I get inspired by what people wear on the
streets. I want to have my own clothing brand.
I want people wearing my clothes.

I recently found a piece that I'd made lying in
a box, behind the closed door of the cupboard.
Discovering it that day rekindled my dreams.

Maryana is in Year 10 at Bossley Park High School. She really enjoyed creating the ceramic artworks for this project and photographing them. To Maryana, being free to fashion means feeling free to wear anything she likes without the fear of being judged. Her signature colours are red, white and black, and the fashion item that defines her style is a short minidress. You will always find her wearing oversized hoodies or tops. And the one thing she will never do: mix patterns!

Maryana remembers a pink floral dress that she had when she was two years old. She really admires the way her mum always adds her own touch to the clothes she buys.

A long-sleeved floral dress and a short crystal vest with a gold or silver chain belt represents her Kurdish culture.

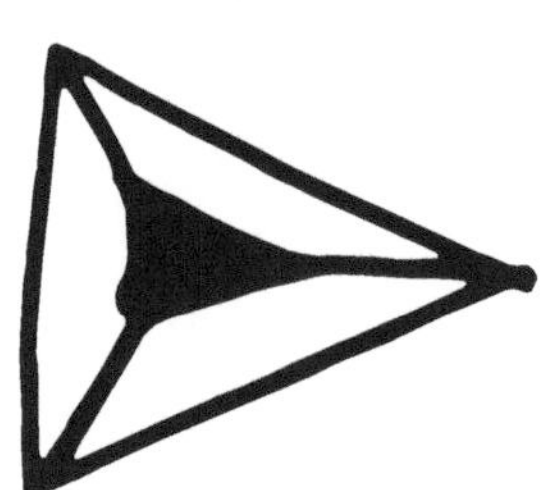

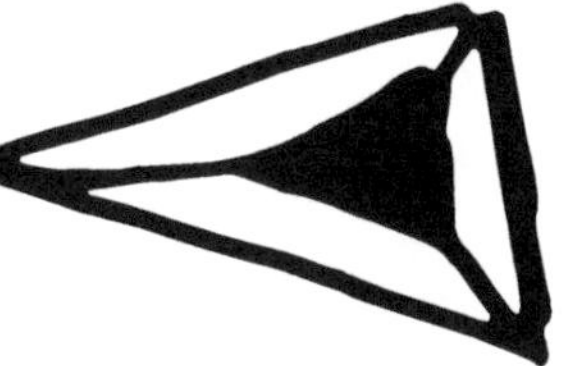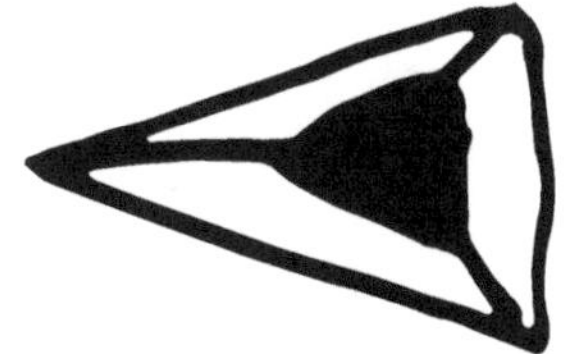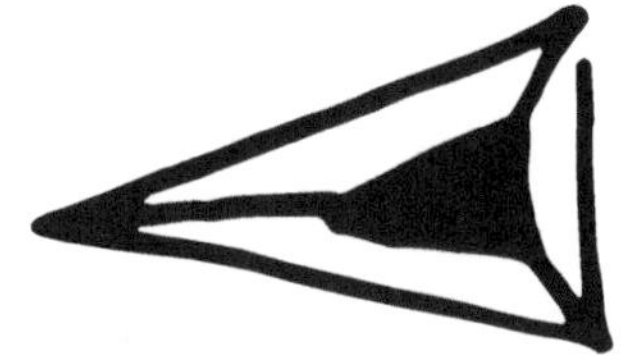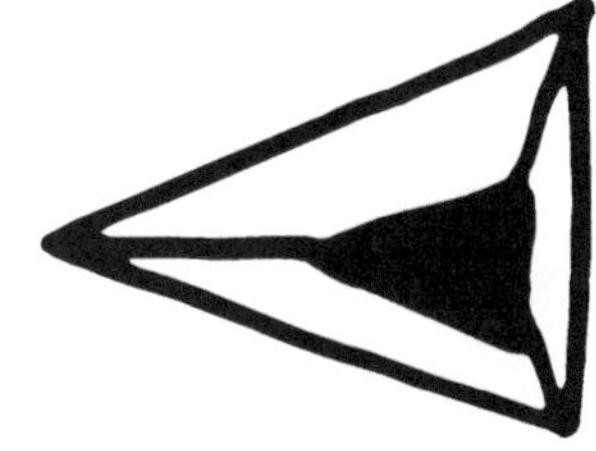

NIGHT CREATURES

A time I associate freedom with is when I'm outside at night watching the stars, hearing the sounds of the night creatures, specifically night cockroaches, distracting me from my thoughts and reality.

MY CHOIR ROBE

A piece of clothing that represents freedom to me is my choir robe. It's a long beige robe with a red collar and borders. It makes me feel free because choir has a big role in the church, especially during events like Christmas and Easter, so it makes me feel responsible. It makes me want to go to church, which helps me build a strong relationship with God.

ant a life amo
time you did s
is never plan
the adventure
is short, liv
happen
nd i

be lost when
omeplace beau
s are calling and
the best dreams happen
ories life is short. liv
st and so the adventur
orn, and time is never
the last time you did
omething for

April is in Year 10 at Bossley Park High School, and she really enjoyed talking to the different creative people in this program. She also liked learning to work with ceramics.

April's signature colours are grey, red, blue and green. You will always find her wearing her black Converse high tops, which she has had for a year or two. They are a little bit worn and the colour is a bit faded, but they look good, they're comfy, and she can wear them with anything (except her school uniform).

April doesn't really care about the world of fashion. She thinks it's a bit weird when people wear something like toilet paper—and call it fashion!

THE BOX

My Grandma shuffled into the room, holding a
large box, leather, and covered in dust. She blew
on the box, getting the dust off. As she opened
it, she revealed a bunch of old photos she'd
kept, as well as a beautiful violet cloth, with
beads and circular sparkly things to make noise.
The photos were black and white, yet I could
see the cloth and all its colour and design.

THE WEDDING

I stood in that huge venue, watching as family
and friends got into a dance circle, wildly
swinging their colourful clothes around, cheering
at the top of their lungs. One of my cousins was
banging a huge drum, the sound booming loudly,
rumbling everyone to their cores. I knew I'd have
a headache in the morning, but right now I was
only focused on the atmosphere of the wedding.

An aspect of Free to Fashion that I enjoyed was making our clay sculptures and making artworks with pastels.

I learned how to design clay sculptures—that was something I did new and learned from Free to Fashion.

To me, being free to fashion means to design and wear any type of clothing and fabric.

My signature colour is black because it matches everything I wear.

The fashion item that best defines me is gold jewellery because it matches my skin tone.

You would never catch me wearing Converse.

BEIGE

My Mum's signature colour is beige. It mixes with her warm honey-brown eyes. It complements her tan skin tone and matches her gold possessions. All eyes shift to her when she steps into the room. Don't get me wrong—her signature colour is every colour she tries on, but it's always that warm beige that stands out the most. I can't even question her every time she steps out in a gorgeous beige outfit, whether it's a dress, shoes, top or pants, because I know she looks amazing. It's her signature colour, and no one can do it better than she can!

JOY

When I think about what it means to be free to fashion,
I think about my sister-in-law. She could make anything
work. Her outfits contrast her emotions kind of like
Inside Out. The way she lays her outfits out the day
before reminds me of Joy. The way she plans her outfits
in her head in a way I couldn't imagine fascinates me.
Give her an outfit that clashes, and I guarantee she
could make it work in a million different ways. When she
enters the room, she shines with colour and heads start
to turn. The way her eyes light up when she finds the
perfect jeans or her size in the pair of shoes she's been
wanting enlightens me. Even though she is limited in
what she can wear she always finds an alternative. Her
outfits are always alive and pop with colour that brings
out her best features. To me she is free to fashion.

SACRED MEMORIES

My signature item is not only an item but a memory, one
I share with my grandma—my baby blanket, a soft pink
Winnie-the-Pooh blanket. It was a gift to me from my
grandma. To me it was more than a gift. I cherished it
and had it by my side everywhere I went. She was always
there for me. Every time the head had a rip, she was there
to patch it up. All those patches unlocked a new memory
until the memories overflowed and all came spilling out of
the blanket with the fluff from Winnie's head. It was time
for the blanket to retire, but my love for her never did.

CRYSTAL

An aspect of Free to Fashion I enjoyed was the opportunity to be more creative and constantly think outside the box.

To me, being free to fashion means having the freedom to express myself through the simple and complex designs of garments (e.g. through hats).

You would never catch me wearing neon and brightly coloured clothes with bold and eccentric patterns.

Fashion and wearables enable me to express my personality, my Chinese culture and choose how I present myself.

HER RUNWAY

Click. Clack. Clack.
My jaw dropped as the woman appeared in front of me. Her white-blonde mini bob with microbangs made her stand out in comparison to everyone else. Her glass-like skin shone in the beaming sunlight. Dressed from top to bottom in Prada, her outfit came with a massive price tag. Still, it was absolutely stunning, like nothing I had seen before. Every path was her runway. Truly amazing, blowing me out of the world. Oh, to see something like that again.

LUCKY GREEN

From basil, sage, gherkin, olive, pine to pistachio—it doesn't matter what shade of green, they're all her favourite! Her bag, clothes and shoes; everything. They all involve a splash of green, a splash of good luck.

She works around the community, helping people with her charm. Everyone is served with peace once they start having a conversation. Her light words can provide comfort and a sense of belonging. Not to mention, just like a four-leaf clover, she is extremely lucky. She's able to predict the next move, always a step ahead of others.

On St Patrick's Day she was decked out in all the shades of green. She was the person with the most lively spirit, always in a great lucky mood.

She is an individual most free to fashion, constantly presenting herself through green clothing, choosing the way she would want to be identified and noticed.

If she didn't wear green, her luck would be lost.

MY EARRINGS

Click. That was the sound the piercing gun made as it punched a hole through my earlobe. The stainless steel earring hugged my ear, yet it didn't make me feel special. 'Here, try these,' my grandma offered. The gold sparkled brightly. It was like they were calling my name. I put them on and instantly loved them. Every time I wear them, they make me feel loved and remind me of my grandma.

My earrings. Where are they? Where did they go? Where is Grandma?

An aspect of Free to Fashion I enjoyed was drawing with pastels to make a design.

Something I did new or learned from Free to Fashion was the process that goes into making a fashion piece.

To me, being free to fashion means expressing myself through fabric or spreading my art through clothing.

My signature colour is yellow. My favourite colour is yellow. I enjoy this colour because of the character Winnie-the-Pooh. I also have a friend called Sunny.

If I could change the world of fashion, I would change how fashion is manufactured and wasted. Leftover clothes not bought would be given to the homeless or people in need.

MY MOTHER'S WEDDING PHOTO

I remember gazing at a framed photo of my mother, glowing in her white wedding dress. My father is standing in his black suit, looking very dapper. It was weird. Seeing my parents look so young and so in love. My mother looked like a porcelain doll, red lipstick complementing her pale complexion, ebony hair in a perfect bun, with delicate strands framing her face. That day I said that I would be just as beautiful as my mother. I would say now I take after my father, but I like to believe that my little sister will at least take after my mother. I'm not mad about looking dapper. Though my older brother takes after my mother, so maybe he will be the pretty sibling. I don't know.

DRESS

I remember wearing an itchy dress. It was a hanbok that my grandmother bought for me when she visited Korea. The skirt was scratchy and the seams kept brushing against my stomach and legs. The skirt rested just below my chest with small straps holding it in place. It felt like I was wearing a tutu as a top. I felt as if I was buried in fabric. The skirt was bright pink and had colourful flowers and butterflies embroidered on it, so I didn't hate it. I just hated wearing it.

It had a small navy jacket to cover the top with long sleeves, all decorated with colourful butterflies and a large Korean word on the clasp of the jacket. It came with a headdress that itched as well, but every time I took it off, a family member would put it back on. They insisted that it was a 'special occasion. It's your sister's first birthday.' I remember protesting: 'But it's not my birthday. Why do I have to wear it?' Me being around preschool age, of course they brushed my protests off, leaving me to sulk in my parents' bedroom. But then I was dragged out by my mother to greet more guests. My only solace was that my little sister wore one too. It was her birthday after all. Looking as if she was drowning in fabric too, I sympathised. Until she cried and had to have her nappy changed. Something about smelly nappies just ruins your appetite. Such fond memories.

BUTTON-UP REFLECTIONS

As I buttoned up my shirt and fixed the cuff on my sleeves, I felt confident, I felt brave and, most importantly, I felt fancy even though the shirt was nothing fancy, just a white button-up collared shirt. In that moment I felt so attractive and cool. I put on some pants and looked in the mirror. In the mirror stood a smart, classy business woman. I pulled my hair into a ponytail. I looked so professional. I switched the pants for a black skirt and gazed at the reflection in the mirror. My reflection changed into a beautiful girl who had just finished working at a cafe. Wearing button-up long-sleeved shirts always makes me feel regal even though it doesn't look like anything special to others. I took off the buttoned shirt and packed it away. My little fashion show had to end.

As I put my pyjamas on and looked in the mirror, I saw my reflection finally show who I truly am. An average girl, getting ready to go to bed. A clumsy, confused girl who hasn't navigated life yet. For now, my reflection will stay as illusions of who I can be. I turn away from the mirror and crawl into bed.

An aspect of Free to Fashion that I enjoyed was the clay work and designing.

Something I learned from Free to Fashion was how fabric designs are made.

To me being free to fashion means creating anything you want.

My signature colour is black because it makes me feel safe.

The fashion item that best defines me is a head scarf (hijab) because I am Muslim.

DRESSES

My idea of being free to fashion is wearing anything you want with complete confidence despite what others might say. I love my dresses, I have a pink one with white flowers, and it's flowy when you wear it. I have a navy one and it trails behind me as I walk. There are so many others and they all represent my identity and show who I am. I love wearing a new dress at every special event, and my friends try to guess what dress I'm gonna wear next. At every event I try to wear a new dress design, with new colours, shades of pink, blues, reds . . . My favourite dress is a rusty pink colour and it has white embroidered flowers. I love my dresses, and I will always wear them.

SHE STOOD OUT

We live in a world where black, brown or neutral
colours are what are mostly worn. I've always
thought that a world like that is boring, but
anxiety took over me, so I never tried to stand
out. One day, like any other day, I went out
wearing my usual black colour palette, when
I saw one woman—she looked like she was in
her 50s—and she stood out! I had never seen
anything like it. Everything she had was yellow.
She stepped out of her yellow car, wearing
yellow leather shoes and a fluffy yellow jumper.
I think you get the point. She was inspirational, I
admired her. Turns out, everyone knew who she
was; they called her the yellow lady.

LEGACY

My signature style is black with a floral
pattern—very minimal, and neutral in colour.

Long ago in Karbala, Iraq, a war took place.
Everyone was in battle. And after it ended, a
new war started.

A woman, oppressed, hurt, was captured and
forced to walk three days under the sun.
But she held on to her modesty.

She held on to it even though they fought her for it.

To protect her legacy today, I wear black like
what she wore.

An aspect of Free to Fashion I enjoyed was showcasing my Iraqi Muslim background by displaying and explaining my country and home garments.

Through Free to Fashion I got to know about how The Social Outfit team gives opportunities to refugees and migrant women.

To me, being free to fashion means to portray my abilities and to feature my individual achievement. Also, it's an opportunity to learn about others' experiences and to establish different cultures through the art of fashion and personal voice.

The fashion item that best defines me is my hijab, as it is a way to identify and represent my Iraqi and Islamic identity.

A YOUNG MUSLIM WOMAN

When I think of being free to fashion, I immediately think of the abilities I can portray, these being the features of my individual achievements. It's an opportunity to express my personal beliefs and self-identity. It allows me to recognise what I am proud of, of seeing others' experiences and speaking of that. Free to Fashion has helped me to establish different cultures through the art of fashion and personal voice. My personal choices of fashion stem from my beliefs, from the meaning of modesty in my religion. I don't find bright colours appealing and avoid showy clothing. A piece of fashion that represents my identity is my hijab, being there to identify me as a young Muslim woman. Free to Fashion has been an opportunity to feel a sense of belonging through personal choices like my hijab.

THE KEFFIYEH

The Keffiyeh, just a square scarf with a simple black-and-white pattern, but it is so much more than that. It symbolises the wise and brave men of Iraq who used to be fishermen in the hot and humid days. It symbolises the trade routes used to transport food and other necessities. It symbolises the courage of my country, my homeland.

Samanta is in Year 10 at Bossley Park High School. She enjoys making ceramic sculptures. She enjoys having the freedom to express herself. Her colours are white, black and green because these colours suit her the best. Dresses define her. She would never be caught wearing skinny jeans, and she will always be wearing rings. She remembers her Don Bosco shirts from childhood. The keffiyeh, which is a square piece of fabric with big sparkles dangling, is the fashion item that represents her culture. It is used in dances at special events like weddings.

DISAPPOINTMENT

It was a random day in 2017 when I woke up thinking about my Don Bosco shirts. It had been ten years since I first got them, but I still had a clear image of what they looked like. I started looking for them. I looked in all the places my mum could've placed them, but I couldn't find them. It felt like I'd lost a part of my childhood, of my past. Feeling disappointed, I went to ask my mum, with little hope they still existed.

DRESS CODE

I had been looking for a dress for my sister's holy communion for two weeks now, when my mother decided to take us to the shops again. We went to store after store because we couldn't find a dress suitable for the dress code. It needed to be modest and suitable for church. I hate looking for dresses especially when they need to follow a dress code, and every store I went to didn't have anything modest enough. I never knew finding a modest dress would be that hard. Until we walked into a store and the first thing that caught my eye was a long-sleeve maxi dress in green. I grabbed it to show my mum and made my way to the changing room. As I pulled the dress over my body, I fell in love with the way it fit my body and how the colour stood out. That was the moment when I figured out green was my colour.

An aspect of Free to Fashion I enjoyed was going to The Social Outfit and seeing their work spaces.

I tried and experimented with oil pastels for the first time as part of Free to Fashion.

To me, being free to fashion means experimenting with lots of different styles and colours, and having freedom.

My signature colour is a nice muted pink or a baby pink, as I love to feel feminine.

The fashion item that best defines me is my hijab as it clearly defines me and my religion.

THE BLUE KNIT

When I think about what it means to be free to fashion, I think about my sister. My sister's fashion inspires me and what I wear. Every time she walks out of her room after finishing getting ready, I always admire her. Whether it is silently in my head or telling her she looks nice—not that she appreciates me. I know she loves when I do, but she can never tell me. One piece of clothing I admire the most is this very nice fitted arctic blue sweater. It matches her blue-themed room, from the cyan blue chair, to the blue and white tasselled bedsheets, to the abstract blue denim rug. When she's wearing the blue top in her room, it makes me happy. It makes my brain smile. It makes me feel peace and comfort.

PURPLE

My sister's signature colour is purple. Ever since I can remember, my sister's room has been themed purple. The colour overtook me as soon as I walked in her room. All the shades scattered across her room—the violet walls, the deep purple chair, and a splash of blue on her desk.

Clothes racks all around us—an array of colours—and my sister straight away moves towards the purple clothing, towards the purple gemstones in her jewellery box.

POP

Walking down the street with my head down, looking at the floor, all of a sudden I see a pop of hot pink from the corner of my eye. I slowly follow my eyes up her outfit to reveal the biggest pop of colour I have ever seen—the bright spring sun shining on her gemstones that are attached all along her bucket hat and the strap of her tote. Head to toe in pink attire.

In that moment, I had no words to describe how she managed to pull off such an outfit, such a colour. She just did!

MILEY

An aspect of Free to Fashion I enjoyed was learning to be creative and creating art from strokes.

To me, being free to fashion means being free to design and create pieces of clothing.

My signature colour is denim blue because it brings out my features.

You would never catch me wearing something colourful.

You will always find me wearing something dark or bright, but not colourful skirts or flares or sweatpants.

Fashion and wearables enable me to express myself and my outgoing personality.

ÁO DÀI

As I held it up, I felt a sense of excitement rush over me.

Áo dài. My cultural clothing is designed with two long pieces. One at the back and one at the front. Long sleeves add to the elegant look of it. The embroidery is amazing—cranes, flowers, all the beautiful things you can imagine are all on there, tying the piece together. Always sewn in red or other bright and loud colours. It makes me feel special, loud. The pants. Silk, straight and simple, making the dress part stand out. It highlights the figure of whoever wears it and complements their features, especially when everyone shows off their personally-sewn ones on Lunar New Year. I've always loved it, ever since I was a kid to now, as a teenager. And I will continue to love it and show it off to the world.

MY COLOUR

Ever since I was a kid I've always loved the colour pink. I loved expressing myself through pink. But as I grew older, I chose not to wear pink or colourful clothes any more. I thought they didn't suit me. However, when I got into high school, I had a teacher who would always dye her short wolf cut something bright and fun. She used that as a way to express herself. I remember her coming to school every month with a different colour—bright red, blue, pink or orange . . . Whenever she did that she looked more joyful, more like herself. She would love to tell us about it.

The way she expresses her bright, colourful self reminds me of when I was a kid, how I used to be, how I used to adore bright colours, how I used to rush to my mum every morning with a new combination of colourful clothes mushed together, and especially how I used to wear them unabashed. I loved colours. Even though I hate how they looked on me. But ever since I met my teacher, I've allowed myself to wear more colours again. Like denim blue. I think it brings out my features. It's made me feel like myself again. Confident.

Athraa is a student in Year 10 at Bossley Park High School. She really enjoyed the experience of working with clay in the Free to Fashion workshops.

Her signature colour is grey because it is close to black. The fashion item that defines her is her baggy jeans: you would never find her wearing skinny jeans or crop tops. You will always find her wearing . . . clothes (just kidding!). It's her rings.

She recalls Assyrian clothes from her childhood. And gold jewellery. She says Arabs mostly like to wear gold jewellery.

WIRE

I can see wired lips,
refugee faces,
the wire shapes of their faces.
They look like they want to say
Help!

This is the story of a woman who
had to try.
To escape.
To leave.

Leaving countries
and houses
that she spent
a life to build.

FREEDOM

Freedom means being able to do whatever I want.
I feel free when I go to the park at night and walk with my music on.
I like to walk alone 'cause it gives me the space I need when I start overthinking,
recalling old memories, imagining my future, wondering about what I will do . . .
Sometimes I feel lost.

Freedom is like a dream.

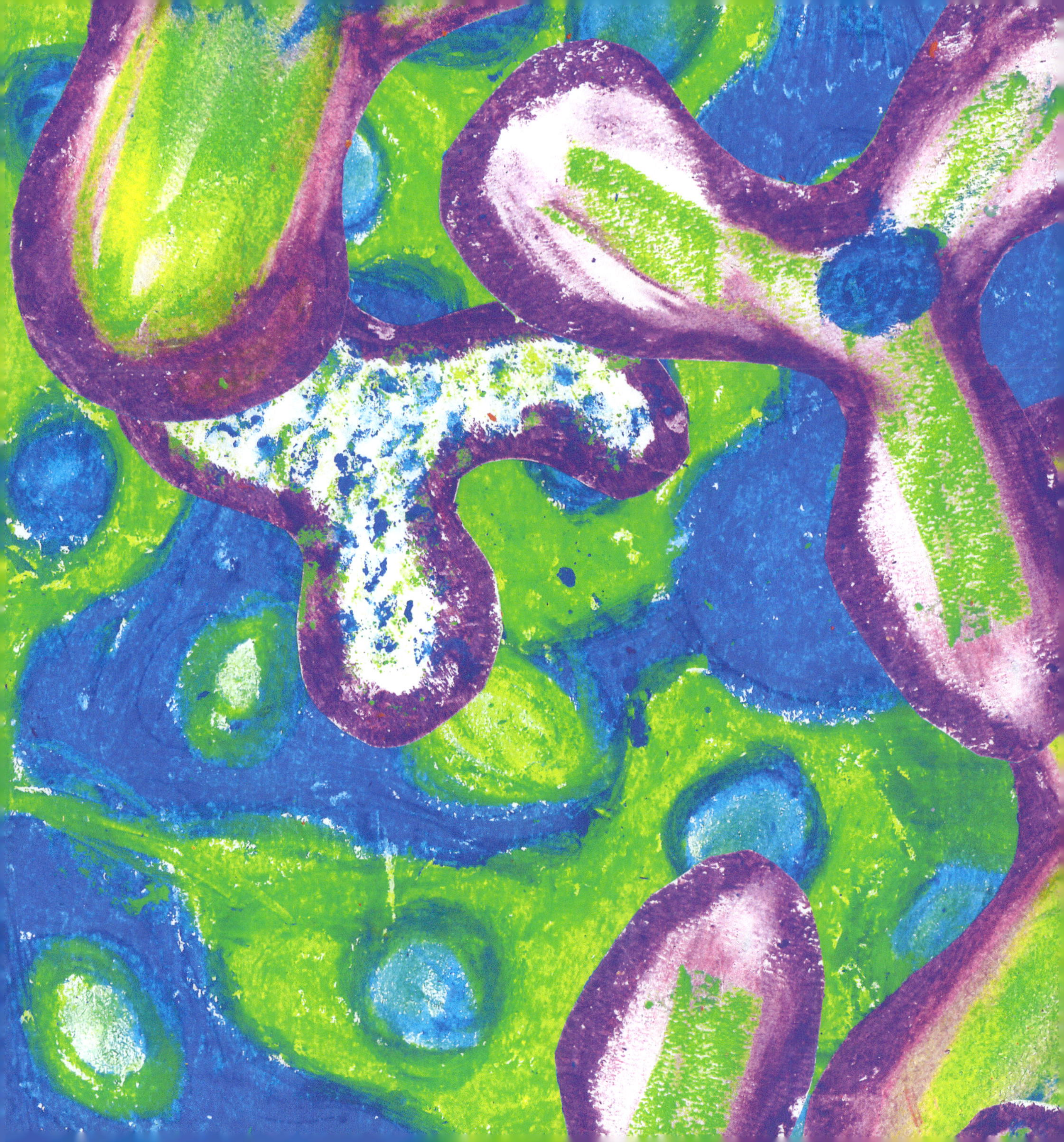

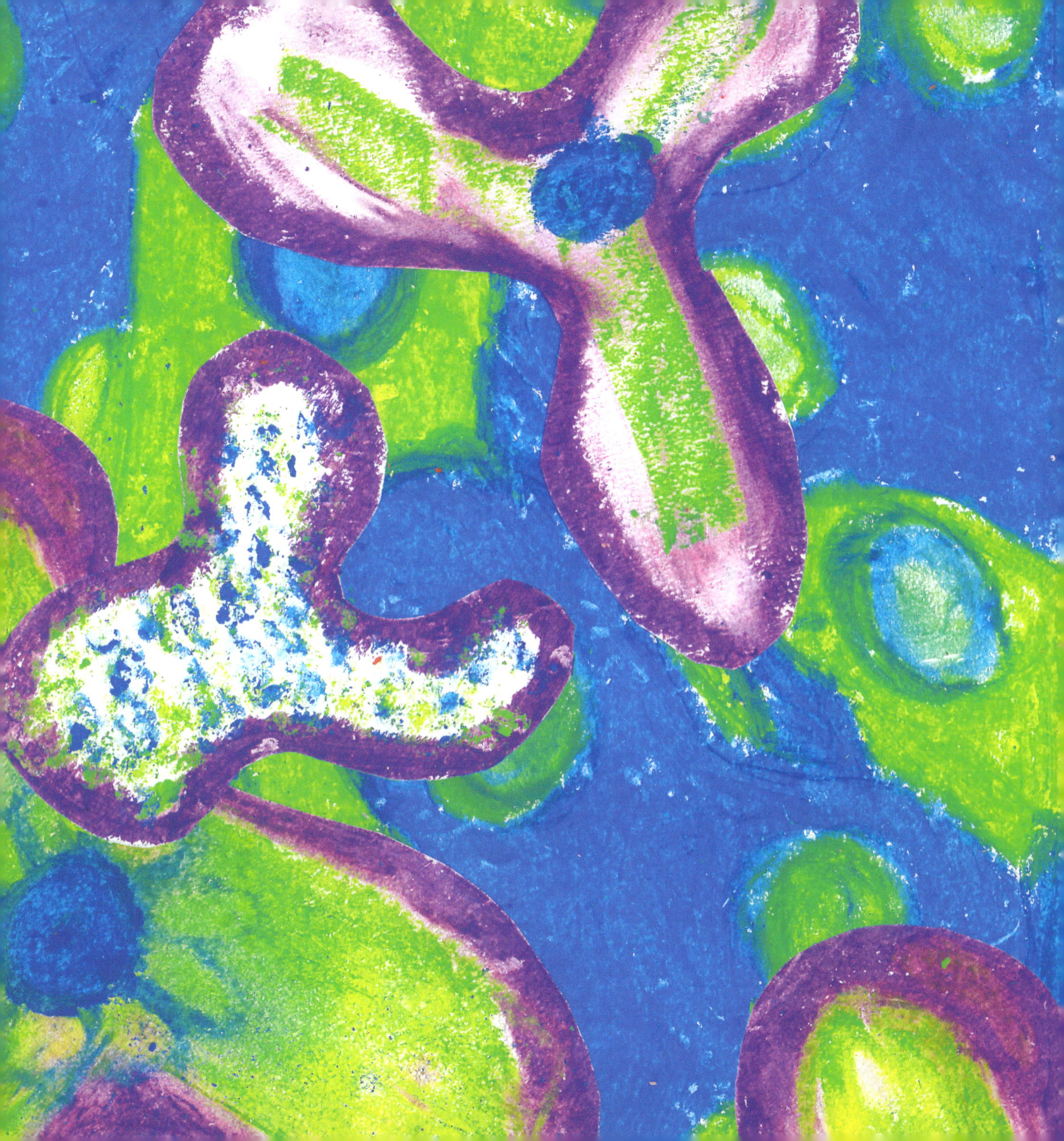

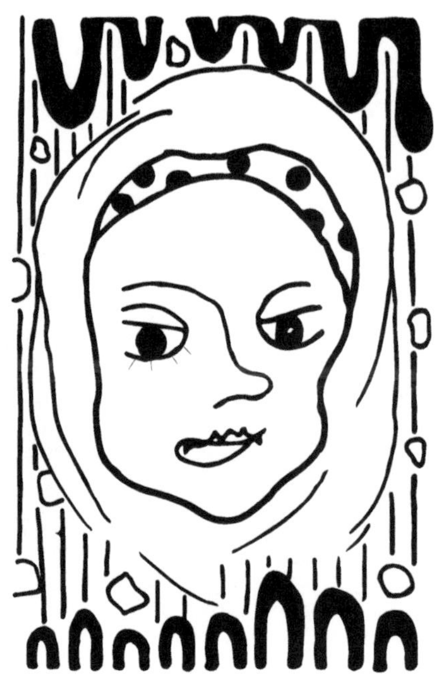

An aspect of Free to Fashion I enjoyed was the clay workshops where Chatcha gave us advice and helped us with our sculptures.

Through Free to Fashion I learned how fashion can create many opportunities for less fortunate people.

To me, being free to fashion means being able to wear what you like without judgement and fear.

My signature colour is 100 per cent green. The posters in my room, my skirts, my dresses, my mug are all the colour of nature. I resonate with it.

If I could change the world of fashion, I would make clothing more affordable and sustainable.

DON'T MAKE ME CHOOSE

Colours . . . blue, green, pink. Which to choose? Everybody has one but me. Maybe purple? Perhaps blue—nope, has to be green. Everybody has one, so why don't I? I should, right? But my closet is mixed like a moody teenager. I like orange, like the sunset; green like the rainforest; or maybe blue like the sparkling ocean. I really don't know. What is my signature colour? Which one is it? I can't decide ...

COLOURS

Walking around has become boring;
everybody wearing black, no colours.
I always felt left out as if I was the lone
sun in a crowd of moons. A star rose, to
shine with me. A girl. Walking with pride
and confidence in all colourful clothes.
A bright yellow blouse, orange pants.
Suddenly my dull light turned bright,
and I was not the lone sun any longer.

HIDDEN JEWELS

'I want those earrings.'

I was referring to my mother's gold earrings that she never wears because they are too valuable.

'One day.'

'One day never comes!'

She opened my hands. 'Today is that day.'

Gold sparkles covered my hands. It wasn't earrings but it was from home.

Rita is a student at Bossley Park High School. During the Free to Fashion project, she really enjoyed laughing and sharing ideas with everyone and messing around with clay. To Rita, being free to fashion means being able to do whatever she desires. She doesn't have a signature colour but chooses colours depending on how she feels on the day. She likes to express emotion through colour.

She remembers a nightdress from her childhood made from such soft and cool material. It was amazingly comfortable, like sleeping on clouds!

BLACK AND WHITE

I'm in trouble. I need to run, run, but
—to where?

I don't belong, like a black-and-white
painting in a gallery full of colour.

I have no home, like a lost puppy.
But at least the lost puppy has somewhere
to go, it has a home when found, unlike me.

Where to go next? New country?
New place? New language?

So lost.

I don't belong in this unfamiliar place,
I wanna go home.
If home was a safe place.

If I had a choice, if my life was not on the line,
I would never leave home.

That's only in my imagination.

To stay in my ordinary house with my
ordinary job in my ordinary life.

Suddenly I must leave everything behind.

THE DRESS OF MY DREAMS

It caught my eye,
plain but extravagant,
simple yet majestic.
A combination of a butterfly
—peacock colour in a
charmeuse fabric.

I wanted it.
I craved it.

With no money in my pocket,
My heart sank.

The dress of my dreams.

So close
Yet so far.

Valentina is a Year 9 student at Bossley Park High School. The aspect of Free to Fashion that she enjoyed the most was the time she spent playing with clay. She learned what ethical fashion was as part of this program. To her, being free to fashion means having the freedom to express yourself, with your personality and your own path.

Her favourite colours are dark ones, like black and brown, or nude. She would never wear bright or neon colours. The fashion item that best defines her is a long silk dress because it, quite literally, defines the shape of her body. You would never catch her wearing boots as they don't suit her. She always wears lashes because they make her eyes look bigger and make her feel more confident. Fashion enables her to express herself and embrace how she looks.

The fashion item she remembers from her childhood is a perfume she wore a lot, and whenever she smells it now it reminds her of the times she used to put it on.

She admires modest clothing as it makes her look more classy. If she could change the world of fashion she would address the need for modest clothes so people can have more options.

The fashion item that represents her culture is a keffiyeh.

FREEDOM

Freedom is hanging out with my
friends at the shops or being home
alone with my cousins. I love it when I
am alone with my friends. I feel like I
am independent and can do anything.
It feels freeing when I'm alone.

Freedom is like a room full of giggling
friends and baking warm cookies,
while watching horror movies.

THE DRESS

My mates and I all went out to look for dresses for a
wedding. We need to find one. We were looking around
all the stores when I stepped into a shop and laid my
eyes on a beautiful, sparkling red dress and immediately
fell in love with it.

'That would look so good on you,' my friend said.

'I'm going to buy it,' I replied.

'Before you buy it, you should try it on,' my friend said.

'I forgot, I'll do that now, thanks.'

I stepped into the dressing room and tried on the dress.
It was a little too tight for me, and while I was taking it
off, it ripped. 'Oh my god!' I was horrified.

'What happened?' my mate replied.

'The dress ripped.'

I asked the staff if they had a different size.

'I'm sorry, this was the last one.'

'It's okay,' I said, dejected.

I was really upset about the dress. But then, the next day,
I went to a different store and found an even prettier one.

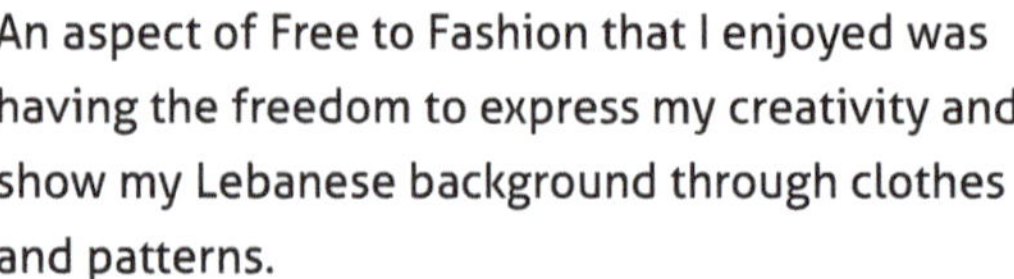

An aspect of Free to Fashion that I enjoyed was having the freedom to express my creativity and show my Lebanese background through clothes and patterns.

Something I learned from Free to Fashion was how emotions can be conveyed through art and design. I learned how The Social Outfit supports refugee women struggling to settle into a foreign country.

To me, being free to fashion means to have the ability to convey thoughts and feelings through textiles and writing. It is a way to connect others' experiences to my own and learn about different communities and lifestyles, such as The Social Outfit, and the authors and artists we met.

You will always find me wearing a hijab. It is also the fashion item that best defines me, because it represents me in different ways and makes me comfortable in my own skin. For example, it represents my different personalities through the different styles and colours I wear. It showcases how I express myself.

HIJAB HELPS

When I think of Free to Fashion, I immediately think about having the ability to convey thoughts through different cultures and communities. I think about some cultures we learned about—Vietnamese, Palestinian—and how they were different to my culture. I loved to see the story of the women who were able to settle in and be stable in a foreign country.

It allows me to connect with different cultures and communities and compare different experiences to my own, to think about how I grew up and the traditions I followed. It allows me to think and reflect on the many mindsets people can have and how they can be portrayed on fabric to show a strong message. Free to Fashion helps illuminate different cultures and countries and inform the world about those. For me, especially coming from an Arab and Muslim background, I dress and act in a different way. For example, I wear a headscarf every day and lower my gaze. I avoid bright colours or attention and even showy outfits. These align not only with my morals but also the values of my religion. Free to Fashion helps people to understand the differences between each other. The hijab is a part of me that will never go away.

BLACK

From as early as I can remember, I have only ever seen my aunty wear black. It got to the point where I would open the closet and see the lightest shade of black to the darkest shade of black.

Black headscarf, black jacket, back pants. Black.

No jewellery. No fragrance. Just all black.

The End.

FOR ME

Clothing for myself. Not because I am oppressed, not for any man. I am not forced but instead I choose to wear what I do for myself, for my god. If I can't pray in it, I don't wear it. Black, the symbol of modesty. The colour that represents me. It reaches my ankle and doesn't show my figure. My skirt.

SUNNY

An aspect of Free to Fashion I enjoyed was . . . everything! I loved getting a chance to explore how art and textiles work together to create beautiful fabric, and creating with clay.

I learned from Free to Fashion that there are many different ways to print on fabric and also how to distinguish between fast fashion and green fashion.

To me, being free to fashion means being able to explore and expand your creativity and blend your personal voice in fashion production without any restrictions.

My signature colours are red, pink and purple. Red, in my culture, is considered a lucky colour. Pink and purple are my favourite colours.

The fashion item that best defines me is my tote bag that has a bear on it. It was a gift from my aunt for returning to Vietnam after three years.

If I could change the world of fashion, I would make high quality garments affordable to everyone, while maintaining a fair pay and work-life balance for workers. Basically demolish Shein.

ME AND MY SISTER

Growing up with my sister, I always held the personal belief that I was less 'cringe' than her. Probably because I never liked watching anime dub, don't use 'skibidi' every five minutes, know when to swear, and don't wear (and like) 'cringy' anime shirts.

Though I am not a big fan of anime, I do follow one specific anime from my childhood. But I NEVER once thought of actually presenting myself out in public with the franchise printed on my t-shirt, as opposed to my sister, who begged my parents to get her *Demon Slayer* and *My Hero Academia* t-shirts once.

Later, I realised that everyone has different preferences, their own style. Some like muted colours on them. Others love to experiment with every single colour at once. Some live in a community that shares a mutual love of cosplay (as animals). It is idiotic to judge people on how they present themselves. There might be a group of people out there that thinks wearing all pinks and having a bear tote bag is 'childish' and 'basic'.

My sister never had 'inferior' taste or clothing style. Our preferences are simply different, and what she wears reflects her interests and personal voice. It is useless to judge and restrict her for liking and wearing anime t-shirts, because she is herself and that is part of her identity. I would be proud to stand next to her. I have to accept it (except for her saying 'skibidi' and swearing uncontrollably).

NOT JUST A DRESS

Áo dài is the traditional Vietnamese dress. It's a part of my identity. Each 'dress' is unique. With intricate patterns carefully sewn to tell stories. There's no gender separation with the dress; men and women are all united. The dress flares downwards, both front and back, creating a modest yet free look. Whenever áo dài is mentioned to anyone who went through high school in Vietnam, they reminisce about their teenage years. A simple white silky dress and pants symbolise the exciting innocence of youth. Not only in school, áo dàis can be seen in festivals in Vietnam, like during Tết, our new year celebration. Streets filled with baih chan, bánh giò, baskets of fruits; red, orange, green, and yellow. Women dressed up in their newest clothes walk the street in vibrant áo dài. The dress is forever imprinted on their mind. The memories it carries of a person's life. Someday, someone will dust one out of the back of the closet and say: 'Remember when . . . '

Áo dài is a part of every Vietnamese identity. It is a part of my identity. The backbone of my culture.

AMPLIFY

ACKNOWLEDGEMENTS

Story Factory and The Social Outfit would like to thank the following donors for making this collaborative project possible:

Barbara Alice Trust
Bianca Spender
Bobbi Mahlab
Cathy Doyle
Deborah Fullwood
Don't Stop Us Now! Podcast
Evelyn Hawkins
Gillian Corban
Johnston Foundation
Julia Ritchie
Kee & Stacey Wong
Kim E Anderson
Robertson Foundation
Snow Foundation
The Office Space